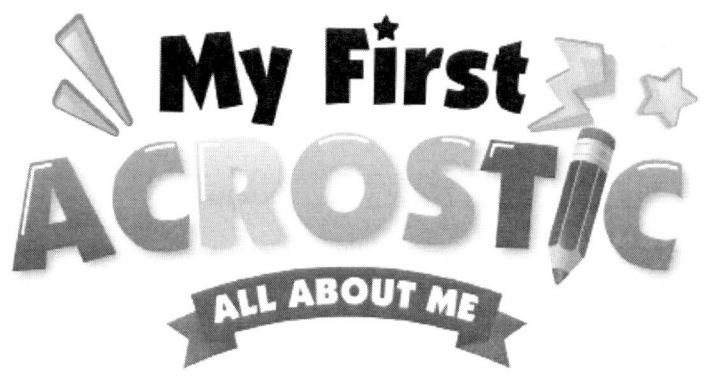

Creative Voices

Edited By Jenni Harrison

First published in Great Britain in 2020 by:

Young Writers
Remus House
Coltsfoot Drive
Peterborough
PE2 9BF
Telephone: 01733 890066
Website: www.youngwriters.co.uk

All Rights Reserved
Book Design by Ashley Janson
© Copyright Contributors 2019
Softback ISBN 978-1-83928-696-4

Printed and bound in the UK by BookPrintingUK
Website: www.bookprintinguk.com
YB0429B

Dear Reader,

Welcome to a fun-filled book of acrostic poems!

Here at Young Writers, we are delighted to introduce our new poetry competition for KS1 pupils, *My First Acrostic: All About Me*. Acrostic poems are an enjoyable way to introduce pupils to the world of poetry and allow the young writer to open their imagination to a range of topics of their choice. The colourful and engaging entry forms allowed even the youngest (or most reluctant) of pupils to create a poem using the acrostic technique, and with that, encouraged them to include other literary techniques such as similes and description. Here at Young Writers we are passionate about introducing the love and art of creative writing to the next generation and we love being a part of their journey.

From pets to family, from hobbies to idols, these pupils have shaped and crafted their ideas brilliantly, showcasing their budding creativity. So, we invite you to proceed through these pages and take a glimpse into these blossoming young writers' minds. We hope you will relish these poems as much as we have.

Contents

Caledonia Primary School, Saltcoats

Daisy Paterson (7)	1
Ava-Rose Amelia Hallam (7)	2
Devlin Cairns (7)	3
Ollie Macleod (6)	4
Connor McFadyen	5
James Marston (7)	6
Millie Padden (7)	7
Ellie Julie Mitchell (7)	8
Emily Rae (6)	9
Sophie Butt (7)	10
Colin O'Reilly (6)	11
Linden Brannigan (6)	12
Holly Bryson (6)	13
Keira-Leigh Conway (7)	14
Rebecca Ball (6)	15
Martha Rose Findlay (7)	16
Isabella Violet MacNicol (6)	17
Alexander McGregor (7)	18
Lola Love (6)	19
Caitlin Suzanne Barr (7)	20
Jacob Taboas (6)	21

Dunn Street Primary School, Jarrow

Ellie Milburn (6)	22
Jake Lugg (5)	23
Ellie Dixon (7)	24
Kara Lugg (7)	25
Sonny Patterson (6)	26
Gracie Dodds (7)	27
Jaeden Alexander Stannard (6)	28
Harry Lee Robert Laing (6)	29

Angel Hosie (6)	30
Ellie-Mae Catley (6)	31
Holly Elizabeth Brook (6)	32
Ronnie Ray Findlay (5)	33
Arlis Avdiaj (6)	34
Alfie Thornton-Grace (6)	35
Connor McGeary (5)	36
Adam Kaminsky (6)	37
Finley Mark Appleby (6)	38
Kayden Davis (5)	39
Tyler George Ward (5)	40
Noah Cartwright (5)	41
Leon Eade (5)	42
Josh Grund (5)	43

Glenbrook Primary School, Bilborough

Hanny Ghobrial (6)	44
Goda Kvietkauskaite (6)	45
Oscar Nawrocki (5), Isla Brown (5), Larra, Demarco Grant (6), Ayaan Mohammad (5) & Isla	46
Eleanor Zanaj (7)	47
Liam Gentile (6)	48
Jack Myers (6), Shiann, Ruby, Harry O'Connor (5) & Sebastian Romaniw (5)	49
Harley Harrison (5)	50

Hydesville Tower School, Walsall

Tianna-Rose Chikwariro (5)	51
Jasmine Kaur Khunkhuna (5)	52
Karina Kaur Sunner (5)	53
Katie Huang (5)	54

Daniel Zachev (5)	55
Rishi Agnihotri (5)	56
Chevéyo Kadii Ngo-Hamilton (5)	57
Jessica Gauden (6)	58
Amar Singh Rajania (5)	59
Armaan Singh	60
Roman Jundu (5)	61
Veer Bahia (5)	62
Taio Caines-Akinsanya (5)	63
Samuel Ball (6)	64
Waris Dhillon (5)	65
Gia Kaur (5)	66

Hythe Bay CE Primary School, Hythe

Felicity Ross (6)	67
Zach Williams (6)	68
Rudy Nelson-Dean (6)	69
Sophie Ward (6)	70
Olivia Biden (6)	71

St Martin de Porres Primary School, Luton

Annabelle Eniola Sebastian (6)	72
Kimberly Iherjurka (6)	73
Richmond Ekwenye (6)	74
Shanelle Grace Castro (7)	75
Annamae Regis (7)	76
Maddox Killeen (7)	77
Amarah Dixon (7)	78
Zakia Bieles Doblas (6)	79
Matthew Foley (6)	80
Jessie Cimeni (6)	81
Estelle Taylor (6)	82
Isabelle Louise Bailey (6)	83
Chisom Onyemekwuru (6)	84
1M Class	85
Olivier Szymanel (7)	86
Gabriel Nascimento Fernandes (7)	87
Amelia Alice Siedlecka (6)	88
Elissa Neo (6)	89

Dewran Dogan (6)	90
Ariana Flutur (6)	91
Jenna Ndubueze (6)	92
Nissi Thompson (6)	93
Zofia Osmanska (6)	94
Ethan Marriott (6)	95
Julia Przeklasa (6)	96
Dawid Malinowski (6)	97
Keeley Tess Baness-Allen (6)	98
Pippa Talampas (6)	99
Nilah Griffith-Nugent (7)	100
Moses Dawodu (6)	101
Osedebamen Okojie-Andrew (6)	102
Tyler Witter (6)	103
Noel Thekkumkatil (7)	104
1P Class	105
Declan Brophy (6)	106

Waterloo Primary Academy, Blackpool

Millie Li (5)	107
Taylan Michael Kucukakca (5)	108
Eadie Wilkinson (5)	109
Jaxon Goulding (5)	110
Kyla-Jayde Moseley (6)	111
Maksims Funikovs (6)	112
Max Curry (6)	113
Myla Julie Newton (5)	114
Jacob Bush (5)	115
Indie-Rose Collier (6)	116
Phoebe Cronin (5)	117
Mollie Whittle (5)	118
Lorelei Riley (5)	119
Harleigh Trask (5)	120
Charlie Lee Inman (5)	121
Jack King (5), Lola, Connor, Jamie, Cody & Willow	122
Eliza Murshed (5)	123
Joey Bancroft (5)	124
Blake Blankson (6)	125
Lilly Lines (5)	126
Harry Stevenson (6)	127
Boe Eric Mallinson (5)	128

Kacey May Donegan (5)	129
Olivia Foster (5)	130
Lily Lynch (6)	131
Levi-Lee Wilkinson (5), Sapphire-Jade & Logan	132
Xavier Jacyno (5)	133
Mia Farrer (5)	134
Alexander Manderson (6)	135
Jake Thompson-Dudson (5)	136
Charlotte-Leigh Withington-McLean (5)	137
James Junior Wallace (5)	138
Jaiden Daniel Singleton (5)	139
Jenson Stones (5)	140
Charlie Alan Wood-Jones (6)	141

The Poems

Gymnastics

G ymnastics is so much fun
Y ippee, when I won a medal
M iddle splits are my favourite
N ever giving up
A nything I can do
S eeing different tricks
T eacher is so kind
I do the splits
C artwheels are so much fun
S cary to do an aerial.

Daisy Paterson (7)
Caledonia Primary School, Saltcoats

Unicorn

U nbelievable flying
N ight-time unicorns have shiny hair
I nside a unicorn, they have a gold horn
C overs things with its horn
O n the cloud, there's a unicorn
R ed, silky horn
N ight, a unicorn turned into a princess.

Ava-Rose Amelia Hallam (7)
Caledonia Primary School, Saltcoats

Football

F ootball is fun
O llie plays against me
O llie beat me at football
T ommy is my friend and I saw him at football
B alls help play football
A lways our team wins
L oads of people go there
L augh when we score.

Devlin Cairns (7)
Caledonia Primary School, Saltcoats

Football

F ootball is fun
O n May, I win a medal
O n football, I win a trophy
T As is near my football
B alls can score a goal
A ll the boys do their best
L ove when we win
L ots of exercise!

Ollie Macleod (6)
Caledonia Primary School, Saltcoats

Pokémon

P okémon is a super game
O ne Pokémon is big
K ing of Pokémon is Pikachu
E ggs are rare
M ewtwo are rare
O ne Pikachu can learn buzz
N ew Pokémon are good.

Connor McFadyen
Caledonia Primary School, Saltcoats

Chocolate

C hocolate is tasty
H ot chocolate is yummy
O pening the wrapper
C adbury is the best
O reos are yummy
L ove chocolate
A fter my dinner
T asty treat
E njoy.

James Marston (7)
Caledonia Primary School, Saltcoats

Rabbit

R abbits are fluffy
A rabbit is fluffy
B ut they are happy
B urrows are the rabbits' home
I t is my favourite animal
T o rabbit, have you been good today?

Millie Padden (7)
Caledonia Primary School, Saltcoats

Blake

B lake is funny
L ion is his favourite animal
A pples are my little brother's favourite food
K ind little boy
E ggs he doesn't like, but he loves Coco Pops.

Ellie Julie Mitchell (7)
Caledonia Primary School, Saltcoats

Lleyton

L oving a lot
L ikes dinos
E verybody in the family loves him
Y ummy snacks he eats
T rains he loves
O n the couch watching TV
N early four.

Emily Rae (6)
Caledonia Primary School, Saltcoats

Sophie

S wimming is fun, I like it
O wls are fun
P ets are funny, and dogs and cats
H elicopters are fun
I ce cream is my favourite
E llie is my friend.

Sophie Butt (7)
Caledonia Primary School, Saltcoats

Mum

D o I have the best mum?
I love Mum to bits
O n TV, she likes to watch me
N ice and kind
N ever be cross
E veryone in my family loves her.

Colin O'Reilly (6)
Caledonia Primary School, Saltcoats

Linden

L ots of people like to play
I like to play
N ovember is my birthday
D inner time, mince, sausages
E very day I am good
N ever afraid.

Linden Brannigan (6)
Caledonia Primary School, Saltcoats

Holly

H olly likes to do gymnastics
O ff to school, I go each day
L ove to run about and play
L ove my family all the way
Y ippee, it's the holiday.

Holly Bryson (6)
Caledonia Primary School, Saltcoats

Dancing

D ancing is fun
A tap dance
N ice teacher
C hildren shuffling their feet
I love dancing
N ew dance moves
G etting fit.

Keira-Leigh Conway (7)
Caledonia Primary School, Saltcoats

Animals

A nimals are awesome
N octurnal animals
I n the forest
M y favourite is
A zebra
L ucky monkeys
S winging in the trees.

Rebecca Ball (6)
Caledonia Primary School, Saltcoats

Martha

M ilk is my favourite drink
A pples are my favourite
R abbits are my favourite animal
T igers I love
H appy every day
A mazing.

Martha Rose Findlay (7)
Caledonia Primary School, Saltcoats

Linda MacNicol

L inda is the best
I n the house, Mum plays with me
N ice mums are fun
D inner times are delicious
A ll the time my mum plays with me.

Isabella Violet MacNicol (6)
Caledonia Primary School, Saltcoats

Racing

R acing is fun
A mazing racing skills
C ars are fast
I win the race
N ice car
G ood, good winning.

Alexander McGregor (7)
Caledonia Primary School, Saltcoats

Ellie

E llie is my friend
L aughs a lot
L oads of fun
I nteresting and kind
E veryone loves her.

Lola Love (6)
Caledonia Primary School, Saltcoats

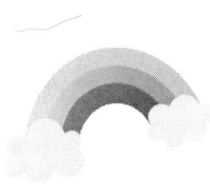

Mummy

M ummy is the best
U nbelievable
M ummy is the best
M ummy is silly
Y ummy food she makes.

Caitlin Suzanne Barr (7)
Caledonia Primary School, Saltcoats

Julie

J ulie is amazing
U nbelievable
L ovely
I think she is amazing
E xcellent.

Jacob Taboas (6)
Caledonia Primary School, Saltcoats

Ellie's Poem

E lephants are my favourite animal
L ove my mum and dad
L ove writing stories
I love unicorns
E llie Dixon is my best friend

M illie is my twin
I love ponies
L ove my dog
B ees are my least favourite
U nbelievable friends and parents
R obbie is my friend
N o sweets for me, I'm grounded.

Ellie Milburn (6)
Dunn Street Primary School, Jarrow

Jake

J ack-in-the-box
A pples
K ites
E lephants

L ollipops
U mbrellas
G rass
G ames.

Jake Lugg (5)
Dunn Street Primary School, Jarrow

I Am Fantastic

   E veryone loves me
   L ove my sisters
   L ove my mum and dad
   I am amazing
   E verything is for me

   D og is the fluffiest in the world
   I love my stepsister
e **X** cellent
   O ther people laugh at me
   N eighbours are kind.

Ellie Dixon (7)
Dunn Street Primary School, Jarrow

Things I Like

K angaroos are my favourite animal
A mazing student
R odents are my favourite toy
A frican snail is our classroom pet

L ily is my friend
U nicorns are pretty
G rass is my favourite plant
G rey is my favourite colour.

Kara Lugg (7)
Dunn Street Primary School, Jarrow

Sonny's Poem

S un gives me power
O ctopuses are one of my favourites
N arwhales are an animal I've not seen
N ice friends never hit other people
Y etis are an animal that lives in the snow.

Sonny Patterson (6)
Dunn Street Primary School, Jarrow

My Favourite Thing

G rapes are my favourite fruit
R acing is my favourite thing to do
A quarium is what I like to do
C ute as can be
I love Mum and Dad
E lephants are my favourite.

Gracie Dodds (7)
Dunn Street Primary School, Jarrow

Jaeden's Diary

J umping is fun
A pples are my favourite fruit
E lephants are my favourite
D inosaurs are the best
E nd of school is my favourite
N ine is my favourite number.

Jaeden Alexander Stannard (6)
Dunn Street Primary School, Jarrow

My List

H ot sunny days are my favourite,
A pples are my favourite fruit,
R abbits are my favourite animal,
R obots are my favourite toy,
Y ellow is my favourite colour.

Harry Lee Robert Laing (6)
Dunn Street Primary School, Jarrow

I Am An Angel

A pple is my favourite fruit
N ow I kind of like chocolate
G reen is my favourite colour
E lephants are my favourite animal
L augh at my friends.

Angel Hosie (6)
Dunn Street Primary School, Jarrow

Ellie

E ating chips is the best
L ove my family
L earn new things every day
I like going to the cinema
E lephants are my favourite animals.

Ellie-Mae Catley (6)
Dunn Street Primary School, Jarrow

Holly

H orses are my favourite animal
O ranges I like
L ollipops are my favourite candy
L augh a lot
Y esterday was my favourite day.

Holly Elizabeth Brook (6)
Dunn Street Primary School, Jarrow

Ronnie

R ats I do not like
O reos I like
N ot nervous at all
N ice to my friends
I like ice cream
E xcited to go home.

Ronnie Ray Findlay (5)
Dunn Street Primary School, Jarrow

Arlis

A lways try my best
R unning with my friends
L ove my mum and dad
I am learning English
S uper tasty pizza is the best!

Arlis Avdiaj (6)
Dunn Street Primary School, Jarrow

I Am Alfie

A mazing
L ove my dad
F antastic handwriting I have
I like snakes
E lephants are my favourite animals.

Alfie Thornton-Grace (6)
Dunn Street Primary School, Jarrow

Kitten

K itten is fluffy
I like it when they jump
T op cat
T ired
E xtra small
N ext to me.

Connor McGeary (5)
Dunn Street Primary School, Jarrow

Adam

A mazing at football
D o my best all the time
A lways learning things
M y mum and dad are my best friends.

Adam Kaminsky (6)
Dunn Street Primary School, Jarrow

Finley

F un to my friends
I ce cream I like
N ice to Ronnie
L ollies
E ggs
Y oghurts.

Finley Mark Appleby (6)
Dunn Street Primary School, Jarrow

Kayden

K angaroos
A pple
Y o-yo
D ad
E ggs
N ets.

Kayden Davis (5)
Dunn Street Primary School, Jarrow

Tyler

T oys
Y ou
L ove my mum
E ggs
R unny.

Tyler George Ward (5)
Dunn Street Primary School, Jarrow

Noah

N ice
O ranges are yum
A pples
H appy.

Noah Cartwright (5)
Dunn Street Primary School, Jarrow

Leon

L ittle
E xcited
O ranges
N ervous.

Leon Eade (5)
Dunn Street Primary School, Jarrow

Josh

J elly
O ranges
S ister
H appy.

Josh Grund (5)
Dunn Street Primary School, Jarrow

Beach

B uilding sandcastles
E ating sugary doughnuts
A rcade games grabbing
C hildren laughing
H ot dog and mushy peas.

Hanny Ghobrial (6)
Glenbrook Primary School, Bilborough

Beach

B oats on the sun
E ating Cornettos
A furry penguin on the corner
C hippy meal
H elicopter.

Goda Kvietkauskaite (6)
Glenbrook Primary School, Bilborough

Hamster

H ungry
A crobatic
M unching
S alad
T reats
E at
R unning.

Oscar Nawrocki (5), Isla Brown (5), Larra, Demarco Grant (6), Ayaan Mohammad (5) & Isla
Glenbrook Primary School, Bilborough

Beach

B ig beautiful sea
E ating ice cream
A corn
C hips
H appy day.

Eleanor Zanaj (7)
Glenbrook Primary School, Bilborough

Beach

B ig blue sea
E asy
A nimals
C razy
H ot sun.

Liam Gentile (6)
Glenbrook Primary School, Bilborough

Dog

D irty paws
O bedient
G orgeous.

Jack Myers (6), Shiann, Ruby, Harry O'Connor (5) & Sebastian Romaniw (5)
Glenbrook Primary School, Bilborough

My Acrostic Poem

C at food
A ffectionate
T ail.

Harley Harrison (5)
Glenbrook Primary School, Bilborough

My Favourite Things

T acos that are crunchy
I gloos that are made out of ice
A pples with big bites
N uts that are hard
N ails that are sharp
A corns that are like chestnuts

R ed velvet cakes that are yummy
O ranges that are my favourite
S old when you move house
E ggs that are runny are my favourite.

Tianna-Rose Chikwariro (5)
Hydesville Tower School, Walsall

My Favourite Things

J is for jelly that wobbles
A is for acorns that squirrels eat
S is for stealing toys in my house
M is for mice eating cheese
I is for igloos, where polar bears live
N is for nice clean room
E is for eyes you see with.

Jasmine Kaur Khunkhuna (5)
Hydesville Tower School, Walsall

Things I Like

K is for Katie, who is my friend
A is for animals I like to stroke
R is for rabbits which are very cute
I is for ice cream I like to eat
N is for Nanny I love very much
A is for apples I like to eat.

Karina Kaur Sunner (5)
Hydesville Tower School, Walsall

All About Me

K nautia flowers make me smile a lot of times
A ll of my certificates are amazing
T ea is my favourite time at home
I love my baby a lot and give lots of hugs
E ach colour of the rainbow is my favourite.

Katie Huang (5)
Hydesville Tower School, Walsall

Things I Like

D inosaurs are my favourite
A fter my lunch, I like playing out
N uts are my favourite treat
I like telling ideas to my friends
E lephants are great
L ions have sharp teeth.

Daniel Zachev (5)
Hydesville Tower School, Walsall

Things I Like

R eal Madrid is my favourite football team
I like playing football
S ix is the number after five
H appy jokes make me laugh
I get changed into my own clothes at home.

Rishi Agnihotri (5)
Hydesville Tower School, Walsall

All About Me

K olkwitzia is a pretty flower
A ll the colours in the rainbow are pretty
D addy sometimes makes cups of tea
I like making things
I like going to the park.

Chevéyo Kadii Ngo-Hamilton (5)
Hydesville Tower School, Walsall

My Favourite Things

J is for jelly
E is for egg
S is for summer
S is for sun
I is for ice cream
C is for caterpillar
A is for apples.

Jessica Gauden (6)
Hydesville Tower School, Walsall

My Favourite Things

A is for alligator and it has sharp teeth
M is for Magnums I like to eat
A is for Alex, my cousin who is ten
R is for Reuben who is my friend.

Amar Singh Rajania (5)
Hydesville Tower School, Walsall

School

S howing off my work
C ooler than ever
H ow fun maths is
O h it's too easy
O n some trips, we go
L earning is fun.

Armaan Singh
Hydesville Tower School, Walsall

All About Me

R ed is my favourite colour
O ranges are good to eat
M ummy, I love her
A pples are my favourite fruit
N uts are bad for me.

Roman Jundu (5)
Hydesville Tower School, Walsall

All About Me

V enom is my favourite toy
E veryone likes playing with me
E lephants are funny to see in the zoo
R unning is my favourite sport.

Veer Bahia (5)
Hydesville Tower School, Walsall

My Favourite Things

T is for T-rex, likes to play
A is for apples
I is for ice cream that is yummy
O is for orange juice.

Taio Caines-Akinsanya (5)
Hydesville Tower School, Walsall

Dogs

D igging in the dirt
O pen the door for them
G oing on holiday with them
S how them you love them.

Samuel Ball (6)
Hydesville Tower School, Walsall

Animals

W is for whales
A is for animals
R is for rats
I is for insects
S is for snakes.

Waris Dhillon (5)
Hydesville Tower School, Walsall

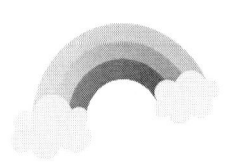

All About Me

G old is my favourite colour
I ce cream is one of my favourite things
A nimals are cute for me.

Gia Kaur (5)
Hydesville Tower School, Walsall

Felicity

F elicity loves her friends
E xcellent at hugging and singing
L ikes crazy stuff to colour
I love Elias, my cousin, she is cute
C ute and cuddly and brave
I love my school, it is good
T iger is my cousin's mascot
Y oshis are one of my favourite toys.

Felicity Ross (6)
Hythe Bay CE Primary School, Hythe

Sprouts

S prouts are yummy
P eople hate them
R eally yummy
O range shaped
U nderneath the green is white
T otally tasty
S prouts are really delicious.

Zach Williams (6)
Hythe Bay CE Primary School, Hythe

Wesley

W es is so cute and lovely
E ver so funny
S o lovely and delicate and
L ovely
E ver so little
Y ummy because he is so cute.

Rudy Nelson-Dean (6)
Hythe Bay CE Primary School, Hythe

Sandy

S andy is our dog
A nd she likes to play
N anny likes to play with Sandy
D addy likes to take her on a walk
Y ou would love her too.

Sophie Ward (6)
Hythe Bay CE Primary School, Hythe

Alfie

A lfie likes to play
L ike a dragon
F ight with a cat
I make my mum stop him
E verybody loves Alfie.

Olivia Biden (6)
Hythe Bay CE Primary School, Hythe

Annabelle

A unicorn is my favourite animal
N ow is time to do my work
N ame all of these people
A beach is one of my favourite places to go
B lue is my favourite colour
E verybody likes to shout in the classroom
L ove your pets
L ove your family
E veryone is quiet now.

Annabelle Eniola Sebastian (6)
St Martin de Porres Primary School, Luton

Kimberly

K imberly is my name
I love my family very much
M ilky Way is my favourite place in space
B read is my favourite breakfast
E lves are my favourite human
R eading books is my favourite thing to do
L oving things is my thing
Y ellow, that's not my favourite colour.

Kimberly Iherjurka (6)
St Martin de Porres Primary School, Luton

Richmond

R is my favourite
I like swimming
C lyden is my best friend
H it the Button is my favourite game
M cDonald's Big Mac is the yummiest burger in the universe
O nly Tyler and Clyden are my best friends
N o means no
D oing games are my best stuff.

Richmond Ekwenye (6)
St Martin de Porres Primary School, Luton

Shanelle

S tones are my favourite things to collect
H ave lots of toys
A fter school, I play
N apkins are what I use for wiping my mouth
E ating is my favourite thing to do
L ike unicorns
L ove ice cream
E at fruits.

Shanelle Grace Castro (7)
St Martin de Porres Primary School, Luton

Annamae

A rabbit is cute and rabbits love carrots
N ext, I love my bunny and
N ext, she loves me and she was cute
A bunny comes to my house
M y very soft bunny
A cat came to my house
E verybody and a puppy came to my house.

Annamae Regis (7)
St Martin de Porres Primary School, Luton

Maddox

M acaroni cheese is my favourite food
A mammoth is my favourite animal
D omino's is my favourite food to eat
D ouble Dip is my favourite sweet
O rbital is my favourite jumping place
X box is my favourite game.

Maddox Killeen (7)
St Martin de Porres Primary School, Luton

Amarah

A fter school, I like having Oreos
M y Lego is fun to play with
A t home I like painting and making slime
R ainbows are nice and colourful
A ll the time my favourite colour is purple
H aving a sister is awesome.

Amarah Dixon (7)
St Martin de Porres Primary School, Luton

Zakia

Z ebras are stripy, not like horses, but have some attitude
A new iPad will surprise me and make me happy
K ittens are loving and cute
I love everything, especially a huge caravan
A nts are very small but super strong.

Zakia Bieles Doblas (6)
St Martin de Porres Primary School, Luton

Matthew

M y life is cool and fun
A ball is my favourite thing
T iger is my favourite animal
T rees are cool
H ouses are my favourite
E very boy likes to be my friend
W hen I go to school I like to sing.

Matthew Foley (6)
St Martin de Porres Primary School, Luton

Jessie

J ust purple is my favourite colour
E very day I love playing with my brother
S undays I like to play on my iPad
S parkly rainbows are wonderful
I love every shiny sticker
E very day I like watching TV.

Jessie Cimeni (6)
St Martin de Porres Primary School, Luton

Estelle

E choes make me happy
S quirmy, melting teddy bears
T ime for lunch
E ggs are my favourite food
L ove is my favourite thing
L ollipops are lovely
E verybody likes each other.

Estelle Taylor (6)
St Martin de Porres Primary School, Luton

Isabelle

I love food
S he is talking on the bus
A bird in the sky
B irds are lovely
E veryone is special
L istening to the horn
L oving life
E very creature is special.

Isabelle Louise Bailey (6)
St Martin de Porres Primary School, Luton

Chisom

C odie Kapow is my favourite program
H orrible Histories has my favourite jokes
I love pizza
S arah is in Bears
O liver is my friend, he's sick
M oses comes to my house.

Chisom Onyemekwuru (6)
St Martin de Porres Primary School, Luton

Garden

G od gives us flowers
A nimals can live in a garden
R abbits can jump in the bushes
D addies can mow the long grass
E ven foxes run about
N ests can be found in the trees.

1M Class
St Martin de Porres Primary School, Luton

Olivier

O ctopuses are very nice
L ike sprinting cheetahs
I love yellow
V isiting my friend is fun
I love Hot Wheels
E ating burgers is fun
R eading books is cool.

Olivier Szymanel (7)
St Martin de Porres Primary School, Luton

Gabriel

G rass is green
A pples are in my garden
B runo is my dad's name
R iding is the best
I love kittens
E very baby is cute
L ove pets especially triops.

Gabriel Nascimento Fernandes (7)
St Martin de Porres Primary School, Luton

Amelia

A bug is my favourite insect
M y friend is Julia
E very day I laugh and play
L ove my family so much
I have been to the park to play
A potato is my friend.

Amelia Alice Siedlecka (6)
St Martin de Porres Primary School, Luton

Elissa

E ating is nice
L earning is fun
I have a big brother
S wimming is fun
S urfing is my dad's favourite thing
A fter school, I like to go to the park.

Elissa Neo (6)
St Martin de Porres Primary School, Luton

Dewran

D elicious cake I love
E very day I play with my friends
W e love science
R unning I love
A nd I go to school every day
N ew toys my mum buys me.

Dewran Dogan (6)
St Martin de Porres Primary School, Luton

Ariana

A jelly is my favourite
R un fast back home
I like chocolate cake
A cat is my favourite animal
N obody playing with me
A tiger eats meat.

Ariana Flutur (6)
St Martin de Porres Primary School, Luton

Jenna

J umping is good because you're exercising
E ating cake is yummy
N avy blue is one of my favourite colours
N aps are amazing
A best day at school.

Jenna Ndubueze (6)
St Martin de Porres Primary School, Luton

Nissi

N oodles are my favourite food
I ce cream is so good
S pice is so spicy and I don't like it
S our candy is so yummy
I ce is so cold and I love it.

Nissi Thompson (6)
St Martin de Porres Primary School, Luton

Zofia

Z ebra is my favourite animal
O ctober is the best month
F is my favourite letter
I love animals, especially zebras
A pples are the best fruit.

Zofia Osmanska (6)
St Martin de Porres Primary School, Luton

Ethan

E nthusiastic elephant Ethan
T ypical Ethan is always typical
H ungry happy haunted Ethan
A lways acting like an apple
N ationally normal Ethan.

Ethan Marriott (6)
St Martin de Porres Primary School, Luton

Julia

J elly is my favourite food
U p, I see at night, I stare
L ollipops are my favourite
I see a cat looking at me
A melia is my favourite friend.

Julia Przeklasa (6)
St Martin de Porres Primary School, Luton

Dawid

D eer are my favourite animals
A mazing yellow flowers
W onderful broccoli is good for you
I love playing on the iPad
D elicious broccoli.

Dawid Malinowski (6)
St Martin de Porres Primary School, Luton

Keeley

K atie and Oliver are friends
E lephants are big
E lephants can't use exits
L ick the ice cream
E yes over there
Y ellow.

Keeley Tess Baness-Allen (6)
St Martin de Porres Primary School, Luton

Pippa

P arties are full of fun
I love my family lots and lots
P izza is delicious
P ets are cute and fun to play with
A unicorn is the best.

Pippa Talampas (6)
St Martin de Porres Primary School, Luton

Nilah

N ice is my favorite
I like my cake upside down
L ollipops are my favourite as well
A bug was in my drink, yuck!
H ats keep me warm.

Nilah Griffith-Nugent (7)
St Martin de Porres Primary School, Luton

Moses

M y favourite food is from KFC
O n the month of May, I am excited
S eeing is wonderful
E ating I love
S pitting is so bad.

Moses Dawodu (6)
St Martin de Porres Primary School, Luton

Deba

D elicious cookies are yummy
E lephants are my favourite animal
B utterflies are my favourite animal
A rabbit comes every Easter.

Osedebamen Okojie-Andrew (6)
St Martin de Porres Primary School, Luton

Tyler

T igers are exciting to play with
Y o-yos are whizzy and fast
L ike playing tag
E ating chips
R eading with Mummy.

Tyler Witter (6)
St Martin de Porres Primary School, Luton

Noel

N ow it is time for lunch
O striches are my favourite
E aster is my favourite eggs
L ist of food is my favourite.

Noel Thekkumkatil (7)
St Martin de Porres Primary School, Luton

Three Little Pigs

     H ouses are strong
     O h no!
yo **U** look tasty
     S tay safe inside
     E veryone lived happily ever after.

1P Class
St Martin de Porres Primary School, Luton

Park

P laying with cars is the best
A robot is great
R ubber is good
K now how to ride a bike.

Declan Brophy (6)
St Martin de Porres Primary School, Luton

Unicorn

U nbelievable
N ice and pink
I nteresting horn
C ute and cuddly
O utside the woods
R eally happy
N aughty sometimes.

Millie Li (5)
Waterloo Primary Academy, Blackpool

Sport

S printing to the finish
P lay my favourite game
O h what a close one
R apid running in basketball
T errific trophies being won.

Taylan Michael Kucukakca (5)
Waterloo Primary Academy, Blackpool

Reuben

R euben is my baby
E very day he smiles
U sually happy
B aby can climb
E verybody loves him
N ice and snuggly.

Eadie Wilkinson (5)
Waterloo Primary Academy, Blackpool

Cheese

C reamy and nice
H appy people eating
E xciting flavours
E xciting to bite it
S tinky and smelly
E asy to eat.

Jaxon Goulding (5)
Waterloo Primary Academy, Blackpool

Maths

M assive numbers to add
A mazing work
T errific teachers to help
H appy children
S miling in every lesson.

Kyla-Jayde Moseley (6)
Waterloo Primary Academy, Blackpool

Sonic

S mily Sonic always
O h how fast he is
N oisy and quiet
I maginative and clever
C razy Sonic guy.

Maksims Funikovs (6)
Waterloo Primary Academy, Blackpool

George

G ood
E xciting
O range colour
R olls around
G eorge is my pet
E xtra special to me.

Max Curry (6)
Waterloo Primary Academy, Blackpool

L.O.L.s

L ovely to play with
O h what beautiful clothes
L ittle shiny L.O.L.s
S miling dolls all the time.

Myla Julie Newton (5)
Waterloo Primary Academy, Blackpool

Snoopy

S noopy is a boy
N ice
O nly yaps
O ften hoppy
P erfect
Y ou are lovely.

Jacob Bush (5)
Waterloo Primary Academy, Blackpool

Pizza

P izza is yummy
I t makes me happy
Z oom to the pizza man
Z esty
A mazing ham.

Indie-Rose Collier (6)
Waterloo Primary Academy, Blackpool

Daisy

D aisy is so cute
A lways happy
I nteresting
S he loves me
Y es, I love her.

Phoebe Cronin (5)
Waterloo Primary Academy, Blackpool

Sugar

S ugar is a dog
U sually happy
G ood girl
A lways kissing
R eally cute.

Mollie Whittle (5)
Waterloo Primary Academy, Blackpool

Tiger

T errible sharp teeth
I am fierce
G rowls loudly
E ats meat
R oars!

Lorelei Riley (5)
Waterloo Primary Academy, Blackpool

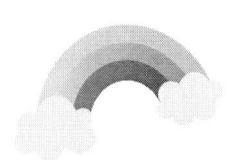

Honey

H omely
O ften happy
N ever sad
E verything cute
Y ou are cute.

Harleigh Trask (5)
Waterloo Primary Academy, Blackpool

Tiger

T eeth are sharp
I n the dark
G reedy
E ats meat
R oars loud.

Charlie Lee Inman (5)
Waterloo Primary Academy, Blackpool

Tiger

T eeth sharp
I n a cage
G rowl
E veryone is scared
R un away.

Jack King (5), Lola, Connor, Jamie, Cody & Willow
Waterloo Primary Academy, Blackpool

Doll

D olls are fun
O nly for me
L ike playing with friends
L ovely and cute.

Eliza Murshed (5)
Waterloo Primary Academy, Blackpool

Worm

W iggles inside the ground
O dd-looking
R ed and brown
M akes no sound.

Joey Bancroft (5)
Waterloo Primary Academy, Blackpool

Cake

C ake is yummy
A mazing icing
K ids enjoy lemon cake
E xciting to eat.

Blake Blankson (6)
Waterloo Primary Academy, Blackpool

Baby

B eautiful girl
A lways smiles
B rilliant kisses
Y ou are perfect.

Lilly Lines (5)
Waterloo Primary Academy, Blackpool

Lion

L ikes to eat meat
I ncredible
O utstanding
N ever go near.

Harry Stevenson (6)
Waterloo Primary Academy, Blackpool

Lion

L oud roar
I n his cave
O n a mountain
N ever fight.

Boe Eric Mallinson (5)
Waterloo Primary Academy, Blackpool

Mum

M um is the best
U nderstanding and kind
M arvellous cooking.

Kacey May Donegan (5)
Waterloo Primary Academy, Blackpool

Worm

W riggly
O n the grass
R ed and brown
M ini.

Olivia Foster (5)
Waterloo Primary Academy, Blackpool

Cat

C ute and cuddly
A lways playing
T ails long and soft.

Lily Lynch (6)
Waterloo Primary Academy, Blackpool

Cat

C ute and small
A ll fluffy and soft
T ail curled up.

Levi-Lee Wilkinson (5), Sapphire-Jade & Logan
Waterloo Primary Academy, Blackpool

Run

R unning is fun
U nder the sun
N ice to win a medal.

Xavier Jacyno (5)
Waterloo Primary Academy, Blackpool

Cat

C ute and cuddly
A lways purring
T otally awesome.

Mia Farrer (5)
Waterloo Primary Academy, Blackpool

Mum

M akes me happy
U sually smiling
M y mum loves me.

Alexander Manderson (6)
Waterloo Primary Academy, Blackpool

Lion

L oud
I n a cage
O n the stones
N ips.

Jake Thompson-Dudson (5)
Waterloo Primary Academy, Blackpool

Cat

C ute animal
A mazing eyes
T erribly naughty.

Charlotte-Leigh Withington-McLean (5)
Waterloo Primary Academy, Blackpool

Mum

M y mum is good
U ltra smart
M akes me happy.

James Junior Wallace (5)
Waterloo Primary Academy, Blackpool

Cat

C ute and cuddly
A mazing animal
T errific.

Jaiden Daniel Singleton (5)
Waterloo Primary Academy, Blackpool

Dog

D angerous
O n a walk
G rowls loud.

Jenson Stones (5)
Waterloo Primary Academy, Blackpool

Rat

R uns fast
A wful
T akes food.

Charlie Alan Wood-Jones (6)
Waterloo Primary Academy, Blackpool

Young Writers Information

We hope you have enjoyed reading this book – and that you will continue to in the coming years.

If you're a young writer who enjoys reading and creative writing, or the parent of an enthusiastic poet or story writer, do visit our website **www.youngwriters.co.uk**. Here you will find free competitions, workshops and games, as well as recommended reads, a poetry glossary and our blog. There's lots to keep budding writers motivated to write!

If you would like to order further copies of this book, or any of our other titles, then please give us a call or order via your online account.

Young Writers
Remus House
Coltsfoot Drive
Peterborough
PE2 9BF
(01733) 890066
info@youngwriters.co.uk

Join in the conversation!
Tips, news, giveaways and much more!

YoungWritersUK   **@YoungWritersCW**